O'DRISCOLL'S TREASURE

O'DRISCOLL'S TREASURE

PATRICK COOPER

Andersen Press · London

For Tara

First published in 1998 by
Andersen Press Limited,
20 Vauxhall Bridge Road, London SW1V 2SA

Reprinted 2004

British Library Cataloguing in Publication Data available
ISBN 0 86264 839 4

Typeset by FSH, London WC1
Printed and bound in Great Britain by Bookmarque Ltd, Croydon

Contents

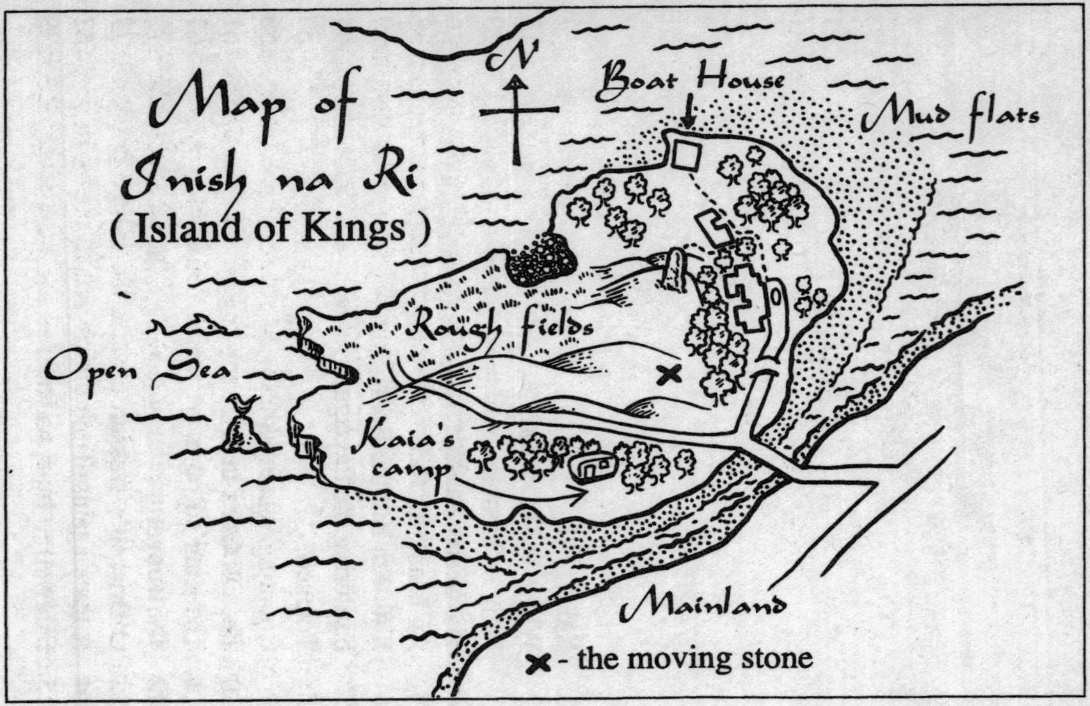

Map of
Inish na Ri
(Island of Kings)
N
Boat House
Mud flats
Rough fields
Open Sea
Kaia's camp
Mainland
x - the moving stone

1
Kaia

I often saw her on the top of the hill next to the standing stone – Kaia, the girl from the travellers' camp. I knew who she was even though I hadn't spoken to her then. She had wild blonde hair, and she was about my age, about eleven.

She'd be standing there, or sitting on a rock, just looking around. But if I came close she disappeared. I knew why she liked being there. You could see all round the bay from the standing stone: the beaches, the big cliffs where the seagulls nested, the ruined castles, and the strings of islands stretching out to the open sea. On a fine day you could sometimes see the Fastnet Rock, a grey tooth on the horizon, which is the last bit of land before America.

It would have been all right if Felix hadn't brought his snake.

Felix and I had a plan. We didn't want the girls, it was just us two. We kept each other awake telling stories until 11.30 p.m. Then we checked that the light was out in Felix's mum's room – not that she'd have heard us, because our room was miles from hers anyway. The house was huge and we were in a different wing.

We slipped down the back stairs. The doors were locked, so we climbed out through the kitchen window.

The woods came right up to the back of the house and it was very dark. I had my torch, a really good one which I'd brought with me from England. But Felix wouldn't let me use it, so we had to creep down the path, feeling our way.

There were lots of noises in the wood, little rustling noises, and my breath sounded loud too. So did my heartbeat. It was quite scary. Then suddenly there was a shriek, and a white shape rose flapping in front of us. I froze.

'It's all right, you eejit,' said Felix. 'It's only an old owl. Come on, now.'

A minute later we were out of the trees and on the soft grass of the hillside. I didn't need my torch now. Above us stretched the Milky Way. I tipped my head back to see it. I'd seen stars plenty of times, but never anything like that – millions and millions and millions of them in a great splash of white, just as if somebody had knocked over a milk jug. They gave easily enough light to see by on the open hillside.

We climbed up to the standing stone. Behind us in the wood the owl screeched again, but it wasn't scary this time.

We'd taken up firewood during the day, so it didn't take us long to make a good fire in the hollow by the standing stone. At first I wanted to pretend being something, like pirates or coastguards. But we didn't need to pretend. It was good enough just being what we were, with the stars and the fire and the stone and the glittering sea.

Felix looked in his rucksack and pulled out a pile of crisps and sweets, and a couple of cans of Coke. He always managed to get hold of junk food. We stuck marshmallows on sticks and burnt them on the fire. They tasted horrible.

Then Felix got out his snake. She lived mostly in a cage in his bedroom that stank a bit because Felix didn't clean it, but he had a cloth bag that he used to carry her around in. She was quite tame. She was called Madonna. She wasn't just a little snake either, she was a three-foot American corn snake.

'She likes the night,' said Felix. 'Lots of snakes wake up at night and go hunting. Do you think she'd catch a little mouse for us if I let her go?'

The snake wound itself round his arm and looked up at Felix as if it wanted to lick him. Or eat him.

'Snakes are very affectionate pets, you know,' said Felix. 'Not everybody realises that.'

I started to laugh. Then I stopped dead, because from the corner of my eye I saw the standing stone move.

'Felix!' I whispered. 'The stone!'

As we both looked, the stone moved again. At least, one side of it did, and then the moving part separated from the still part and became Kaia, the hippy girl.

She stepped down over the rim of the hollow, so that the firelight shone on her gold hair. She was looking intently at Felix.

'I want to look at the snake,' she said. She had a London voice, a bit like mine, sounding flat next to Felix's singsong Irish.

Felix eyed her suspiciously.

'You'd be scared to touch her, I'd think,' he said.

'Don't be stupid,' she said. 'I'm not scared of snakes. It's not poisonous, is it?'

'Might be,' said Felix.

He uncoiled Madonna from his arm and pointed her head towards Kaia. The snake moved slowly round the edge of the fire, as Kaia squatted down.

'Don't move now,' grinned Felix. 'If you frighten her, she'll bite yer.'

Kaia gently stretched her arm out. The snake coiled round it, liking the warmth. Kaia lifted her up towards her, touching the scales with the fingers of her other hand.

'It's not slimy at all,' she said thoughtfully. 'Wish I

had one. There aren't no snakes in Ireland, or I'd catch one. I had a lizard once, but the dog got it.'

She sat down, and Madonna moved across from one arm to the other, and then, quite abruptly, started to head slowly off Kaia's lap and out into the night, as if she sensed something out there to eat.

Felix picked her up.

'I'll have her back now,' he said. 'Don't want her escaping and terrorising the neighbours.'

He eased Madonna back into her cloth bag. He fumbled in the dark with the drawstring then pushed the bag into his rucksack. Then he offered Kaia some of his Mars bar.

'I don't eat that rubbish,' she said. 'Rots your teeth and gives you spots.'

Felix pulled a face.

'You sound just like my mum,' he said. 'What are you doing here anyway?'

'I could ask you that,' said Kaia.

'This is our home,' said Felix. 'We live here.'

'So do I,' said Kaia.

'You don't,' said Felix. 'You're just squatters.'

Kaia said nothing. She just looked at him, and Felix started looking at the ground and biting his nails, like when his mother told him off and he knew he was in the wrong.

'I'm only visiting anyway,' I said, feeling awkward. 'I live in London.'

'Yeah,' said Kaia, still looking at Felix. 'London, I used to live there too.'

She got up and stood at the rim of the hollow, looking out towards the sea.

'We won't none of us live here soon,' she said suddenly. 'You know what's going to happen, don't you? People are going to buy all this whole island, our wood, that big house you're living in, and all. They're going to make it into a holiday camp with a golf course and a marina. We'll all have to go.'

'You're telling a lie,' said Felix sharply.

'Everybody knows. All the adults know. It's all the adults talk about in the bars. I go there with my dad, and I hear it. How this big company called "CountryClub" is buying Inish na Ri for a million pounds. You ask your mum. She knows. She just hasn't told you. We'll all have to live somewhere else then. Somewhere horrible probably.'

She turned to go. Then she looked back at us.

'If you let me hold the snake again tomorrow, I'll show you something else you didn't know.'

She vanished into the night.

We soon went home after that.

Back in our bedroom, Felix opened his rucksack and pulled out Madonna's cloth bag.

The drawstring was loose, and the bag was empty.

2
Where is Madonna?

Felix and I have known each other since we were small. His mother, Mary, was an old friend of my mum, and they'd been to stay a few times in our house in London, and we'd been to see them in Ireland. But it was the first time I'd stayed there on my own.

Felix had two sisters called Sarah and Jessie. Felix pretended to hate them, but he didn't really. Sarah was thirteen, and Jessie was six. Sarah was like another mum for Jessie, because Mary was always busy doing a million things. They spent most of their time with the pony, Sugar. I'd have liked to learn to ride myself, but Felix didn't want me to.

Their dad had died in a boating accident three years before, and I knew from my mum that they'd had a hard time since. They'd had to move house a lot, and they didn't have much money. They'd come to Inish na Ri less than a year before, as caretakers. Inish na Ri was perfect, I thought. The perfect place to live.

We were late getting up next morning.

'Listen, you lot,' said Mary as we ate our cornflakes. 'Sean rang up last night and he's coming down to stay. I don't want the house in a total tip. You can start by tidying your rooms, then we'll do the rest of the house. And that means now.'

'All right,' nodded Felix, with his mouth full. But as soon as Sarah and Jessie went upstairs, he tugged my arm.

'Come on, Chris,' he said. 'We've got to find Madonna.'

And before anyone could see us and tell us not to, we were running through the wood, and back up onto the hillside.

We found the remains of our campfire in the hollow, but there was no sign of Madonna, which wasn't surprising. Snakes don't leave many signs. But we thought we'd better search, so we set off round the hill in opposite directions.

'Remember to look under things,' shouted Felix. 'Snakes hide under stones and that.'

There were a lot of places for a snake to hide among

the big rocks and gorse and heather. I didn't see much point, but I wandered around for a bit. Then I sat on a rock near the top, and looked round the island. There was a plume of smoke from the wood where Kaia's family lived. And I could see the hump-backed bridge that joined the island to the mainland. The tide was low, seagulls were poking about on the mudflats.

Felix gave up too, and came and sat next to me.

'I've got an idea,' he said. 'We'll leave a pinkie near the campfire, as a sort of bait. Maybe she'll come and eat it while we're not looking and then we'll know she's there.'

Pinkies are frozen baby mice. Felix kept a bagful of them in the freezer to feed Madonna, and he had one thawing out in his pocket. He put it in the hollow, next to the ashes of our fire, and then we went down to the beach and turned over stones, looking for crabs.

I suddenly remembered about tidying our room. We must have been ages just mucking about, and I thought we should go straight home before we got into trouble. But Felix had to check first whether Madonna had taken the pinkie.

Kaia was in the hollow. She held up a limp, pink corpse.

'What's this? Looks like a dead alien!' she said.

'That's for Madonna,' said Felix. 'We lost her up here last night. She must have just pushed out of her bag. But she's got to be around here somewhere.'

Kaia opened her eyes wide.

'A beautiful snake like that, and you lost it! What are you going to do? You can't just leave it roaming loose in the Irish countryside. You'll have to tell somebody.'

'We'll find her,' said Felix quickly. 'She won't be gone far. Probably hiding in a hole round here, most likely. I hope she's all right now.' He glanced out to sea where black clouds were moving in, ready to swallow the sun. 'She won't like it if it rains...'

'Can you keep a secret?' Kaia interrupted him.

We both nodded.

'Do you promise?'

'Of course we do,' said Felix.

'Cross your hearts and hope to die?'

'Cross my heart and hope to die,' we each said, folding our arms across our chest.

'Then I'll show you something. It might have gone there. You never know.'

'What are you talking about?' asked Felix.

'Shut up and I'll show you,' said Kaia.

She led us to the side of the hill, where we could see the roof of the big house straight below us among the woods. There were lots of slates missing.

Kaia stopped suddenly.

'Nobody else knows,' she said. 'The old man showed me.'

'What old man?' I asked.

'You know, the old geezer who lived here. The one that died.'

'Mr O'Driscoll,' said Felix.

'That's it. He was a good old bloke. It was him that let us on the land here. We were beside the road before that, hassled by everybody. People used to throw their rubbish at us out of their cars, things like that, you wouldn't believe it. My dad said he couldn't take any more, we'd have to go back to London. But the old bloke used to stop off and chat to my dad about horses and things, and then he said we could come and camp in his wood. My dad thought he was brilliant. He said he was descended from the old kings of Ireland, that he was the last Irish king. I think he was joking, but I'm not sure.'

Felix was looking impatient. 'Come on,' he said. 'What are you going to show us?'

'Keep your hair on,' said Kaia. 'This is important, see? Because he showed me, see, and nobody else knows. He used to come up here, and I used to talk to him sometimes, because he was all right, and he showed me this place and he said his treasure's down there. That's why you have to promise not to tell anybody, and it's serious.'

'Get on with it,' said Felix. 'We've already promised, haven't we? And what's it to do with my snake anyway?'

You'd never have found it by accident. We had to push through gorse bushes, and even then I wouldn't have noticed it – a slab of rock with tufts of moss and grass growing off it. Then I saw the carving on it – gouges and spirals, the marks of the ancient people who lived here thousands of years ago.

Kaia spread her arms across it.

'You have to hold it a certain way, and it turns,' she said. 'I can't do it by myself. One of you go the other side.'

Felix gripped the stone opposite her and started to heave. Kaia stopped.

'You're pushing too hard,' she said. She looked at me. 'You have a go!'

I held the stone, feeling for handholds.

'That's it,' said Kaia. 'Just feel it. Shut your eyes and feel it.'

I shut my eyes. The stone felt big between my arms, but my fingers found details in the grain, until they were comfortable. Then quite suddenly the stone seemed to vibrate. It was like a deep singing, like a whale song.

'Turn!' called Kaia softly.

Almost of itself, the stone lifted and turned.

Felix drew his breath in, and I opened my eyes. Beneath us, rough steps were cut from the rock, leading to a small passage about three feet high, which disappeared into darkness. Its walls were damp, and covered with lichens and moss.

'That's a souterraine,' said Felix. 'There's loads of them round here. The ancient people made them to store their food in when they were attacked. I've learned about it in school. Do you think Madonna's down there then? She might be. She'd like it in there.'

'Let's go in,' I said.

Felix didn't look so keen. 'It's a bit dark, isn't it? What's in it anyway? O'Driscoll's treasure?'

'I've been in a little way,' said Kaia. 'But it's really dark and scary. I thought I'd get stuck or something. The old man wanted me to see how far I could get, said I'd find something. But I couldn't go, not by myself. Then I didn't see him again.'

Felix was gazing into the passage. 'I'd say an adult would have to squeeze to get in there at all,' he said. 'Nice place for a snake though. I thought I might have seen Madonna's little eyes glinting at me just now.'

'I'll get my torch,' I said. 'It's a really good one.' And I jumped up and ran down the hill to the house.

'Oh there you are,' said Sarah, spotting me as I ran in. 'Where's Felix then? You'd better get him here double quick. He's in serious trouble. I don't know what he's done, but Mum's furious!'

3
Felix in Trouble

I ran back up the hill and told them. Felix looked worried.

'We'd better go,' he said. 'We'll meet here later, right?'

'When?' asked Kaia.

'Depends on my mum,' said Felix doubtfully.

At that moment a gust of wind splattered rain against our cheeks.

'It's going to rain,' said Felix. 'We'll come when we can.'

He put the pinkie on the steps, and we slid the stone back into place. Then the rain started seriously, whipping in off the sea. As Felix and I ran down to the shelter of the house, I looked back and saw Kaia standing by the stone with the rain lashing around her, watching us go.

The kitchen was always warm, with its rusty old coal stove and clothes hanging to dry from a rack on the ceiling. The old dog, Jasper, lay in his smelly basket in one corner, and the cat was in the other corner, in a cardboard box with four little kittens. We weren't allowed to pick them up yet, because they were too small, but they squeaked all the time. There was a hamster too, in a cage on a shelf, but it only woke up at nights.

The kitchen window looked out onto an old shed. One pane was cracked. Most of the windows in the house had cracked panes – and there were a lot of windows: 36 or 37. I'd been counting them.

By the time we got there, the whole family were sitting round the kitchen table waiting for us.

'You, Felix!' said Mary. 'I've been looking for you. You're in trouble, you are.'

Felix sat down at the table. He didn't say anything.

'You were told to tidy up,' she went on. 'Have you seen what your room looks like? Chris's half is all right, but yours is like a pigsty. It's disgusting. And your snake's cage stinks. If you don't keep it clean you won't be allowed to have a snake. Got it?'

'Yes,' said Felix quietly, looking at the table, probably relieved that she hadn't noticed his snake wasn't even there.

'And about that snake,' his mum continued. 'You've been carrying it about with you, haven't you? You're not to do that. If it escaped there'd be hell to pay. Keep it in its cage from now on.'

I thought Felix should have told her then, but he wasn't like that.

'Can I have a bit of bread?' he asked.

'I haven't finished yet,' said Mary. 'It's not just Sean who's coming. Kathleen and Desmond are coming too. I want the whole house really clean and tidy, and that means everybody doing their bit. And I want you to behave properly towards Kathleen and Desmond too. Be polite, like you can be. No practical jokes this time.'

She looked hard at Felix, who went on studying the table. Last time she came, Kathleen had found a big dead spider in her bed. Felix swore it wasn't him, but everyone suspected him.

Kathleen, Desmond and Sean were between them the owners of Inish na Ri, since old Mr O'Driscoll died. He'd left it between them, because they were his only relations. Sean was the one who had most to do with the house. He was an old friend of Felix's family, and had asked them to live there as caretakers.

'It's about selling the house,' said Felix, up in our room. The rain was rattling on the window panes.

'It's bound to be,' he went on, stuffing some old trousers into a drawer. 'They wouldn't all come together otherwise. They hate each other, actually. Maybe that girl's right. Maybe they've sold it already.'

He looked out at the rain.

'Jeez, I hope Madonna's all right. It's wild out there. I reckon she'd be snug enough in that souterraine though.'

When we'd finished our room we had to clean the rest of the house, and it was quite a job with all those corridors. The house was big rather than grand, and really shabby, but there was a huge staircase with heads of dead animals hung in it, like you see sometimes in old films. The best of these was a wild boar, with big tusks going brown with age, a bristly nose and a nasty look in its eye. Its mouth was half open, as if it was about to take a snap at someone.

'The old boar's haunted,' said Felix as we cleaned the stairs. 'There's a curse on it. You have to treat it with respect. On full moon nights it'll come alive and chase people it doesn't like, and bite them probably.'

We finished our cleaning, The rain had stopped, and we were just about to slip off up the hill again, when we heard Sean's car rattling over the cattle grid. So we waited to see him.

He was big and bald and good fun, and sat back in the kitchen, joking with Felix's mum, and cutting big chunks off a fruitcake for us.

'How's the snake, Felix?' he asked.

'She's fine,' said Felix with his mouth full.

'Where is she?' asked Sarah suddenly.

'She's sleeping,' said Felix. 'She's shedding her skin.

You don't want to disturb a snake when she's shedding her skin.'

Sarah looked unbelieving.

'I'd like to see her though,' said Sean, standing up. 'Is she up in your room? Let's take a look...'

'I'd rather you waited till tomorrow actually,' said Felix coolly. 'If you don't mind.'

Sean sat down again.

'Okay,' he said simply. 'Don't let her escape, mind,' he added. 'Not with my cousin Kathleen coming. Kathleen's absolutely terrified of snakes. Desmond wanted to keep one when he was a kid, but Kathleen raised the roof about it, so he couldn't. I wouldn't even tell her you've got one if I were you...Talk of the Devil! Here they are.'

The cattle grid clattered again, and Sean and Mary hurried out to greet Desmond and Kathleen.

Felix nudged me.

'Come on,' he said. 'Let's go!'

But Sarah was watching us. 'Where are you going?' she asked sharply.

'Just going,' said Felix.

'Can we come?' asked Jessie, who was always on for something exciting.

'You've lost your snake, haven't you?' said Sarah. 'You should tell Mum.'

'Can you not see I'm busy?' said Felix. 'Come on, Chris!'

Sarah blocked his way.

‘We’re coming with you,’ she said. ‘I want to know what you’re up to.’

‘We’ll look for Madonna with you,’ said Jessie.

I thought Felix might hit Sarah, so I slipped between them.

‘The thing is, it’s a secret,’ I said. ‘We’ve made a promise and we’re not allowed to tell you yet.’

‘You *are* onto something, aren’t you? Okay, I’ll give you till supper. If you don’t tell us then, I’ll tell Mum about your snake.’

4
The Secret Passage

The rain had stopped, but there was no sign of Kaia on the hill.

'It doesn't matter about her,' said Felix. 'We can open it easily without her.'

We went straight to where we thought the tunnel entrance was. We thought we knew exactly, but we couldn't find it at all. In the end we gave up, and crouched in the wet grass looking out at the sea, which was flecked with white horses.

'We'll have to find Kaia,' I said. 'Shall we go to her caravan and see if she's there?'

I wanted to see where Kaia lived, but Felix snorted.

'Walk into that lot? We'll be covered in fleas in five minutes.'

'Don't be stupid,' I said. 'Kaia's a lot cleaner than you are.'

'She's not,' said Felix. 'Anyway, I'm not going down into that nest o' thieves.'

'You're the bloody thief! And a liar! And a dirty smelly skunk at that!'

It was Kaia. She was standing right behind us, eyes blazing.

Felix jumped up and turned on her.

'I'll give you one for that!' he said, launching himself at her.

Kaia just stepped aside and caught him with her arm as he rushed her.

Felix went flying. But he was up in a moment and flung himself furiously on her, pulling her down with him onto the wet grass.

Felix was bigger than Kaia. It looked as if he would easily get the better of her. But Kaia was quicker and stronger than she looked, and she could time things. She slipped out from under him. Felix got up and tried a big kick, but she just whisked aside and caught his leg and tripped him – and a moment later she had him face down on the turf with his arm twisted up behind him.

'Say you're sorry!' she said. 'Say you'll wash your mouth out with soap and water for those stinking lies.'

'Help me, Chris!' called Felix. 'Come on, you're my friend!'

I didn't move. Kaia twisted his arm tighter.

'Say it! Say you're an idiot and you'll never speak those lies again.'

'She's right,' I said. 'Better say it!'

'All right,' said Felix. 'I'm a stupid eejit, and I'm sorry, and will you please let go of my arm now...'

She still didn't let go, though.

'And just remember if you try anything back on me, I'll find that snake of yours and I'll skin it and send you the entrails.'

That was a really good threat, I thought, just like a gangster movie.

'Will you let me go?' gasped Felix.

She let go and came and sat beside me.

'What do you hang out with him for? He's a lying prat.'

'He just says things,' I said. 'You shouldn't take any notice.'

Felix was rubbing his arm, and grinning. One thing about Felix, he never held grudges.

'You know a bit about fighting, don't you?' he called over to Kaia. 'Where did you learn it?'

'From my dad,' she said. 'He'd teach you too, if you weren't so stuck up.'

Felix looked interested, but he said nothing.

'What about this tunnel?' I said. 'If you've finished fighting. That's what we came up here for, remember.'

'I watched you looking for it,' said Kaia. 'You didn't have a clue, did you? I was going to show you, but I don't feel like it now. You can try and find it again yourselves, but you won't. The old man put magic on it to stop people finding it. I'm the only one who knows it now.'

Felix came over to us.

'Show us,' he said. 'If we find Madonna, I'll let you hold her.'

'I don't feel like it,' said Kaia.

'Oh, come on,' said Felix, 'this is serious. My sister's said she's going to tell on me this evening. I've got to know if Madonna's there. At least we'll see whether she's eaten the pinkie.'

'That's your tough luck,' said Kaia. 'I should think you'll be in a lot of trouble when your mum finds out how you lost your snake and all.'

'I'll have to tell them about the tunnel,' said Felix.

Kaia jumped up.

'You made a promise! I'll kill you if you do that!'

'Shut up, both of you,' I said. 'It's getting late. We haven't got much time. Look, I've got my torch with me. Show us the tunnel, Kaia. Please!'

She shrugged, and then she led us straight to the flat stone. It was easy; I don't know how we didn't find it before. We turned it aside, and looked down into the passage again.

The pinkie had gone.

'She's taken it!' said Felix. 'She's down there all right.'

'Let's go and look!' I said. I switched on my torch,

and swung myself down onto the steps. I had to bend almost double so as not to hit my head.

It was really tight in the tunnel. They must have been small, the people who made it and used it all those years ago.

'Come on,' I shouted. 'It's a bit creepy, but it's okay!'

The others didn't follow, though. They just peered in after me.

'Look out for Madonna!' called Felix.

At first I was half crawling down that little tunnel, but then it opened out a bit and I could walk hunched over. I went slowly on down, feeling my way on the stone floor. It was very silent down there. Then the beam of my torch picked out a low doorway in the side of the tunnel. I bent over and peered in, flashing my torch around. There was a little room: its roof too low to stand up in, some pebbles on the floor, a rock in one corner and a musty smell. But nothing else – at least, nothing I could see.

I went on down the passage, which was getting slowly higher, though I still couldn't walk upright. It turned a corner, so I couldn't see the light of the entrance behind me any more. And then it ended in a wall of rough rock. But just before it ended there was another low doorway. This time I knelt down and squeezed through it, and found myself in a room much like the other, only bigger. I could stand upright. And there was a long flat stone in the middle of it, like a table. But otherwise it was the same: mould on the walls, and water dripping somewhere. No snake. No treasure. Not even any old bones. Just darkness and a bad smell.

I flashed my torch around, and it made weird shadows.

In the silence I felt my own heartbeat, and suddenly I got scared that the others had shut the door and left me there. I turned and hurried stumbling back up the passage.

It was a relief to see Kaia and Felix still peering in after me. I pushed myself out, glad to breathe the fresh air.

'There's nothing in there,' I said. 'Just a passage and some caves.'

'There can't be nothing,' said Kaia. 'The old man said his treasure was down there.'

'Have a look yourself,' I said.

'I know my snake's there,' said Felix. 'She was probably hiding. But she ate the pinkie.'

'Anything could have eaten the pinkie,' I said. 'But why don't we all go in? It's scary by myself.'

They both looked doubtful.

'We need another torch,' said Kaia.

'And someone to guard the entrance. It wouldn't do if it shut itself when we were inside.'

'Okay,' I said, 'I've got a plan. It means bringing in Sarah and Jessie, because we need more people and then they won't tell on us. So we make them swear like we did. Then tomorrow morning we organise a proper search. Right?'

To my surprise, they both agreed.

5
An Island for Sale

That evening we sat in the library after our tea. We didn't usually sit there – only when there were special guests. The adults were drinking whiskey. We were just sitting and listening.

It's interesting listening to adults talk sometimes. Even if they are a bit boring and don't always make sense, they know a lot of things we don't know, and if you just stay quiet enough, they forget you're there. So we stayed quiet. Jessie was looking at a picture book, and Sarah and Felix and I just flopped back on the sofa.

'He was a bit of a queer fish, Uncle Michael...'

It was Desmond talking. He had a big red face with a

moustache. He and his sister Kathleen had driven over from London together.

'. . . We always thought he was loaded. All those rumours about the Crown Jewels stacked away in the cellar. Turns out the house hasn't even got a cellar. And poor old Uncle Michael hadn't a bean!'

'What do you mean, the Crown Jewels?' asked Mary.

'Just a tall tale,' said Sean. 'You see, in the old times before the English, there were local Kings and a High King and they'd be elected from among the chiefs of the clans. Our family is descended from the O'Driscoll chiefs, so some of our ancestors could have been Kings of Munster, possibly even High Kings of Ireland.'

He paused, and sipped his whiskey.

'And then the family's always been involved in the resistance against the English, one way or the other. There were tales of secret societies meeting on the island, gatherings of the chiefs, that sort of thing. Carrying on the old ways. So when he was drunk, Uncle Michael sometimes got into wild talk about being in the line of the High Kings of Ireland, and people joked about his Crown Jewels. It was all just bar talk. Nothing in it.'

'So which of you'd be the King now?' asked Mary, looking between Desmond and Sean.

'Search me!' said Desmond. 'There'd have to be a gathering of the chiefs and an election . . . but none of us are male line, so that counts us out. Still, I expect there's plenty of O'Driscolls in County Cork willing to take up the title for a pint of Guinness!'

He guffawed. Nobody else joined in.

'How old is the house, then?' asked Mary.

'Hard to say,' said Sean. 'It was built on the ruin of an O'Driscoll castle that was destroyed in Cromwell's time, and they used the same stones. This is the old part, where we're sitting now. You can see how thick the walls are. Then they kept adding wings. A lot of it was built by my grandfather who made a lot of money in Africa. But one way or the other, I'd say there's been an O'Driscoll lived on Inish na Ri for over a thousand years. Until now, that is ...'

'Until now!' echoed Kathleen. She wore earrings and a lot of make-up. She was smart. Too smart for that house.

'Drink to Uncle Michael O'Driscoll, shall we?' said Desmond raising his glass. 'And to the Crown Jewels we all wish he'd had!'

They drank. Then Mary noticed us, and sent us to bed. The adults went to the kitchen for their supper.

Sarah came and sat at one end of Felix's bed. She looked like she meant business. She had long black hair which she usually plaited, but now it was hanging round her shoulders. She looked really pretty and very determined.

'What's going on?' she asked. 'Why haven't you told Mum your snake's missing? You're only going to get into worse trouble when she finds out. And what are you up to on the hill?'

'It's like this ...' said Felix. And he told them about

the midnight feast, and Kaia, and Madonna going missing. When he came to the secret passage, though, he stopped.

'This is a secret,' he said. 'And it's not our secret either. If I tell you, you have to swear to keep it.'

So we swore them to secrecy, like Kaia had sworn us, except that Felix added a bit on, so they swore:

'Cross my heart and hope to die, in the name of O'Driscoll and the High Kings of Ireland.'

Jessie loved it. Sarah looked as if she found it a bit silly, but she swore anyway.

When Felix had finished telling them everything they sat for a moment thinking about it.

'Will you come up with us tomorrow?' I said. 'We need more people to explore it properly, and more torches too. Kaia thinks Mr O'Driscoll's treasure is in there, but I couldn't find it on my own – we need a proper search party.'

Jessie jumped up and down in excitement.

'Oh goodie, goodie, goodie!' she said. 'I can't wait! Can we go now?'

Sarah got up and took Jessie's hand.

'We'll go in the morning,' she said. 'Come on, Jess. I'll read you a story.'

At the door, she turned again to Felix.

'They're talking downstairs,' she said. 'You know what it means, don't you? They're chucking us out. We're going to have to move again.'

*

As soon as Sarah and Jessie had gone, Felix jumped up.
'Let's go and listen,' he said.

We tiptoed down the corridor, because the floorboards made a noise when you trod on them, and into the bathroom. The bathroom was straight above the kitchen and it had big cupboards, which connected down to the kitchen below. You could sit inside them and hear every word from the kitchen, as clear as if you were there.

Kathleen was speaking.

'Whatever way you look at it,' she said, 'we have to sell. The house is in the most frightful state. It needs thousands – no, tens of thousands spending on it, just to stop it falling down. There's those dirty squatters in the far woods, too. How are we ever going to get them out? CountryClub can deal with all that, and their offer is very good indeed. No one else will offer us half that sum.'

'But they're going to pull the whole house down,' said Sean. 'They're going to cut the woods. Build a golf course over the hill. Make a marina where the boat house is . . .'

'You're just being sentimental, Sean,' said Kathleen. 'It's progress. A lot of people would really enjoy those things.'

'Progress,' echoed Desmond, who sounded like he'd been at the whiskey.

'Anyway,' said Sean, 'I promised Mary when they moved in that the caretaker's job would be for at least five years, and you both agreed to that at the time. Are we going to break our promise?'

'We'll be all right,' said Mary softly.

'We'll make it up to you, of course,' said Desmond. 'It really is a very good offer, you know. And they're not going to wait.'

'Uncle Michael will be turning in his grave,' said Sean.

'Then he should have made more sensible provisions, shouldn't he?' said Kathleen sharply. 'He's left us no choice.'

'There is one possibility,' said Mary. 'You see, this house could easily divide into smaller units. You could borrow money from the bank to make half the house into holiday cottages, leaving a flat for yourselves to come and stay in when you had a mind, and a cottage for us so we could stay on as caretakers and look after the lettings for you. Then you could let the land out at a proper price, and maybe do up the boathouse. It's a bit of work, true, and there's no instant riches like the other way. But you'd get to keep the house and put a bit of life into the place without ruining the whole thing.'

'I think that's a good plan. I think we should consider it,' said Sean.

Kathleen laughed sarcastically.

'Shall we have a vote on it?' she said.

They moved back to the library after that, and Felix and I went to bed.

'One thing,' said Felix. 'With all this going on, Mum's never going to notice about Madonna. Jeez, I miss her. I hope we get her back tomorrow.'

We fell asleep.

We hadn't been asleep long when the screaming started.

6
Kathleen and the Boar

We jumped out of bed and ran into the corridor. Lights were coming on all over the house.

'It's the boar,' said Felix. 'He's chasing Kathleen. He doesn't like her.'

We reached the big staircase and, sure enough, Kathleen was standing near the top of the stairs, staring at the boar's head. She was wearing a nightdress and she'd got her make-up off, and she was white. Sean was beside her, and he put an arm round her.

'What happened, Kathleen?' he asked. 'What's the matter?'

She pointed at the boar.

'That thing . . . it . . . it . . . it stuck its tongue out at me!'

It was hard not to laugh. I saw Sean wanted to laugh too, but he controlled himself.

'It can't have done, Kathleen. It was just a trick of the light,' he said.

'I hate this house,' said Kathleen venomously. 'It's creepy, creepy, creepy. I hope it *is* pulled down.'

I glanced up at the old boar as she said that, and the funny thing was, I thought I saw a glint in his glass eye, as if he was even angrier than usual.

Then suddenly Kathleen started screaming again, a series of high whoops that could have taken off the ceiling.

Everyone was there by now. Desmond and Mary clustered round Kathleen trying to calm her, and little Jessie with her eyes full of sleep stared at Kathleen open-mouthed.

But Felix and I were watching the boar.

And in the shadowy light of the one electric bulb in that huge stairway, it did look as if the boar's tongue was moving. Almost as if he was trying to speak, or maybe take a snap at us.

Then, as we watched, the tongue grew longer, thrust itself between the boar's tusks, and turned into a banded corn snake.

'Oh my God!' Kathleen stopped screaming, drew her breath in, and held it. She wasn't white any more. She was green.

She backed away up the stairs, keeping her eye fixed

on Madonna, who was hanging from one of the tusks and nosing around, looking for a way down.

'Felix!' said Mary in a deep voice that sounded cross – until you saw her eyes, which were twinkling.

Kathleen reached the top of the stairs, turned and fled into her bedroom, slamming the door. Desmond followed her.

The vibration from the door banging seemed to bother Madonna who pulled herself back up and disappeared surprisingly quickly into the boar's mouth.

'I'll get a ladder,' said Felix, racing down to the kitchen. He was back in a few moments with a stepladder, put it up and climbed up to the boar. He held on to its tusks for balance.

'Careful!' said Mary. 'And don't stick your hand in. You'll get bitten.'

Felix took no notice. He peered into the boar's mouth.

'There she is,' he said. 'I can see her eye glinting at me. Come on, dear, I'll put a nice little mouse to warm on the stove for you.'

He put his hand gently onto the boar's tongue and waited a few seconds. Then we saw Madonna's head come out, and she wound herself slowly up his arm.

Felix climbed down the ladder, with his snake held safe, and a big triumphant grin.

'There's nothing to smile about,' said Mary, still trying to be fierce. 'Put that snake back in its cage, Felix, and make sure it's locked properly. Then come down to the kitchen. In fact you may as well all come to the kitchen. I think we're all well awake by now.'

Felix had to explain himself. Mary probably thought he'd organised the whole thing on purpose just for the fun of frightening Kathleen. Perhaps she hoped he had in a way. But Felix told her that Madonna had escaped from her bag and he'd been looking for her everywhere and hadn't dared tell anyone. He didn't mention that he'd lost her in the middle of the night up by the standing stone, but it was the truth otherwise, and Mary accepted it.

She gave us all a biscuit. Then Sean came down and she put the kettle on. Jessie cuddled up to Sarah, and we all sat around in our dressing gowns. It was nice.

She'd just made the tea, when Desmond came in. He looked embarrassed. He said Kathleen was in her room crying hysterically, and that she said she couldn't stand it any more in the house, she wanted to move to a hotel.

Mary poured him a cup of tea.

'There's nothing we can do now,' she said. 'She'll have to find herself a hotel in the morning.'

Desmond sat down and drank his tea. It must have been a lot nicer in the kitchen than being upstairs with Kathleen crying.

Then he started talking to Felix about snakes. He told him how when he was a boy, he'd always wanted to keep a snake, but he hadn't been allowed to. So Mary let Felix run upstairs and bring down Madonna, and he fed her a pinkie. Desmond was thrilled, watching her swallow that little pink mouse, and the bump moving slowly down her throat. Sean was bending over to watch too. They were just like a couple of kids. Then Madonna started to wind herself up Desmond's arm. He sat there with a big grin all over his red face, while she slid round his neck and into his hair. The rest of us were laughing.

At that moment Kathleen walked in.

She didn't stay long. She looked around us, and caught Desmond's eye and saw his hair. I thought she was going to scream again, and I could see Felix putting his fingers in his ears, ready. But she didn't. She just turned and walked straight back out.

Desmond's face had gone even redder. He unwound Madonna and gave her back to Felix. Then he followed Kathleen.

'Well,' said Mary gently, 'I think it really is bed-time now.'

Upstairs, Felix put Madonna carefully in her cage. We lay down and put the lights out.

'That was a good one with Kathleen,' said Felix, chuckling in the dark. 'Did you notice, I didn't even get punished at all.'

There was a long silence. I was drifting off to sleep.

'I'm blowed if I can work out how she got into the old boar, though,' said Felix suddenly. 'She couldn't climb down, so how did she climb up? And how did she come to be in the house anyway?'

There was another silence.

'We'll look into it all in the morning,' said Felix.

A moment later he was snoring loudly.

7
Exploring the Passage

A lot of things happened the next morning. The first thing was that Desmond drove Kathleen off to the local town to find a hotel. I saw her sitting in the car. Her face was like a stone.

Then, while we were still finishing our breakfast, a man came to the door. He talked to Mary, and then he talked to Sean, and then he went away.

'Who was that?' asked Sarah.

'Just a fellow who wants to poke about a bit looking at old stones on the hill, nothing really,' said Mary.

Anyway, the weather was nice again. Sarah and Jessie

hadn't forgotten about exploring the tunnel, but they had to clean out their pony first, so Felix and I went ahead to meet Kaia.

As we got out of the trees behind the house, we could see the hill and the standing stone above us. There were two people there. One was Kaia. The other was the man who'd come to the door that morning.

We hid behind a gorse bush and watched till the man had gone. Then we ran up the hill.

'Who was that?' asked Felix.

Kaia looked serious.

'He nearly found the tunnel,' she said. 'He found the stone. He was looking at all those funny marks on it. I went and talked to him to get him away from it, and he started telling me things. He said it was his job looking at old stones and that, and finding out what had gone on in the past, and he thought this island was once a really important place, and those marks were a part of it. I told him about Mr O'Driscoll being descended from the old Kings of Ireland, and his treasure and that. He laughed, but he was interested. He said he was something – an oli . . . an 'ologist . . . '

'Archaeologist,' I suggested.

'That's it. He's all right. He knew about all the people who lived here before us. He said in the old days people lived more like we do, in our camp, and they didn't leave many marks. He works out how they lived from bits of things he finds in old fireplaces. Bits of old bone and that. I half wanted to tell him about the tunnel. He'd have been really excited. But he might find it in the end anyway.'

'I thought you said it was magic,' said Felix.

'Yeah, well there's magic and magic,' said Kaia.'He might know it. He knows a lot of things.'

At that moment Sarah and Jessie arrived, breathless from running up the hill.

'Have they sworn?' asked Kaia, looking at me. I nodded. But we all swore again to be on the safe side. Then Kaia led us to the stone.

We clustered round the stone, and Kaia and I pushed it open.

Jessie and Sarah gazed down the steps into the tunnel.

'It's very dark,' said Jessie. 'Can we go in?'

Felix was sitting back on some heather chewing the end of a piece of grass.

'You go down,' he said. 'I'll keep a look-out.'

I looked at him and suddenly realised he was scared to go in. Before that I'd never thought Felix was scared of anything.

'Oh no you don't,' said Sarah. 'You go in with us. Jess'll keep a look-out, won't you, Jess?'

Jessie's face fell.

'I want to go in,' she said.

'Don't you want to see for yourself what's in there?' I said to Felix.

He shrugged. 'We need a good look-out.'

'You're scared, aren't you?' I said.

'It's not that,' he said. 'I just thought I'd let you lot go...'

Jessie was already climbing down the steps.

'Let him stay,' said Kaia. 'He's just a coward, that's all. Anyway, we'll find the treasure, so it'll be ours.'

'Oooh, it's really dark,' said Jessie excitedly from inside.

'Come on,' said Sara. 'Who's got torches?'

I went in the front with Jessie. Jessie could stand upright, and she wasn't scared at all, just excited. Kaia was right behind me. I could hear her breathing – everything sounded loud down there – and if I stopped she bumped into me. Sarah came at the back. She had a good torch, and Jessie had a little one.

We flashed our torches around the little room, and then went straight on to the further chamber, with the big flat stone.

'Maybe there's cave paintings,' said Sarah, shining her torch carefully up and down the walls.

Kaia borrowed my torch, and found some cup and ring marks and spirals on the flat stone. In the far corner there was a pile of rocks as if some of the roof had fallen in.

We weren't finding much, but it was fun.

Suddenly Felix called down to us.

'Hey, watch out,' he said, trying to keep his voice low, but still be heard. 'That man's coming back!'

We hurried back along the passage to the steps.

'He's coming straight towards me,' said Felix urgently. 'It's too late to come out now. I'll shut the stone up till he's gone. You've got a good hiding place anyway.'

'Ooh,' said Jessie. 'We're going to be locked in!'

She jumped up and down in her excitement. She was the only one of us who could jump up and down. The rest of us were bent over by the roof of the tunnel.

Felix pushed the stone back and we were in the dark.

'I don't like it,' said Kaia softly behind me. 'It gives me the creeps being shut in like this. Suppose we never get out, or run out of air, or something like that. We shouldn't have done it.'

'Move back,' I said. 'Let's give ourselves a bit of space.'

Kaia had my torch. She turned, crouched down and crawled into the little room.

We hadn't really been in there before, just flashed our torches in as we passed. The ceiling was low, and there was only about enough room for the two of us. Kaia knelt on the pebbly floor, flashing the torch nervously at the ceiling. I sat on a rock in the corner.

She flashed the torch at me and laughed when I blinked in the beam.

'Funny,' she said. 'When I came before, when the old man sent me, I got really scared. But it's all right now. It's still creepy, but I don't feel scared with you.'

Then she shone the beam on the rock I was sitting on.

'Hey,' she said. 'That rock – it's all covered in them marks!'

I knelt next to her and we looked together.

'Shine the torch down the back of it,' I said.

We bent over the rock with our heads nearly touching and peered down the gap between the rock and the wall. It was only a little gap, just a couple of inches. But we could see clearly through it, and what we saw made us gasp.

Behind the rock there was a crack in the wall of the cave, just about big enough to squeeze through. And on the other side of that crack we could see stone steps, leading down.

We had discovered the entrance to another tunnel.

8
Trapped!

Felix was calling from outside.

'He's gone. You can come out now!'

Kaia and I pushed along the tunnel to join the others. Jessie was shining a torch and Sarah was pushing at the stone from underneath.

'Come on, Felix,' she said. 'Move it. It's stuffy down here. We're running out of air.'

'I'm pushing as hard as I can,' Felix called back. 'I think it's jammed.'

'Ooh,' said Jessie. 'We're trapped in the tunnel! We can't get out! The air's going to run out! And I bet there's ghosts of old kings, too. And snakes probably.'

She waved the torch about excitedly.

'Hold on, Jessie,' I said. 'Hold the torch steady for us, will you?' I pushed past her, and up behind Sarah. There was a chink of light on one side of the stone, where there was a little gap, and I thought, that's how Madonna got in, through that hole.

Sarah said, 'You have a go, Chris. I can't budge it.'

She squeezed back past me and I went up to the top of the steps and put my shoulder against the stone.

'One, two three, heave!' I shouted through to Felix.

Nothing happened at all.

'Are you pushing?' I called through.

'I am,' said Felix. 'She won't budge.'

'Felix, you'll have to get an adult,' said Sarah. 'Get that man back. He could do it easily.'

'My torch batteries are running out,' said Jessie. 'Ooh, we're going to be left in the dark!'

It was true, her torch beam was dimmer, though mine was holding out.

'Wait! You're doing it all wrong! Get out of the way, Chris!'

It was Kaia. Sarah moved back to let her pass. I came down the steps and she squeezed past me.

'Listen, Felix,' she said. 'Use your brain for a change. You don't just push it. You put your arms round it, and feel those funny marks with your fingers. Got that? Then when I say so, you twist and lift at the same time... Chris, shine your torch here a minute.'

She started to feel all over the underneath of the stone,

till her shoulders were almost flat against it, and her hands splayed out on either side, her fingers finding cracks or marks to grip against.

'All right,' she called up. 'Now let's move it!'

For a moment nothing happened. Then quite suddenly, as if on a groove, the stone slid smoothly back, and Felix was grinning down at us.

We piled out and threw ourselves on the grass.

'That was brilliant! Can we do it again?' said Jessie.

We lay on our backs on the grass watching the clouds scudding across the sky.

'What did the man want?' asked Sarah.

'Dunno,' said Felix. 'He just smiled and said hello, and walked on past. He stood at the top of the hill for a bit, then he went down the other side, towards the beach.'

Kaia got up and went up the hill to look. She was back in a moment.

'He's down at the bottom of the island,' she said. 'Miles away.'

I wasn't sure whether to tell them then what we'd found but Kaia blurted it right out. Suddenly everyone was sitting up and listening – none of us had really thought we'd find anything.

'Let's get back in and have another look,' said Kaia. 'We might shift that rock that's blocking it, between us.'

'I vote we tell the man,' said Sarah. 'He'll know what to do, and he'll be really pleased. And we can still claim the treasure!'

'Eejit!' said Felix. 'Once the adults get hold of anything they just put fences and signs saying KEEP OUT!'

'I'm going to have another look,' I said, getting up.

'Me too!' said Jessie.

Kaia was already at the entrance.

'Felix can play look-out again,' she said, 'since he's too scared to go in.'

Felix went red.

'Shut your face!' he said. 'Chris, give me your torch.'

He pushed past Kaia, and set off down the steps into the tunnel. His hand was shaking a bit, holding the torch, but he managed it.

'Don't anybody shut the stone this time, whatever happens,' said Sarah.

We all tried to cram into the little cave, and Felix shone my torch behind the rock.

'Jeez, you're right,' he said. 'That looks an awful small hole, though. Come on, Chris, let's give it a heave.'

The two of us tried to get a grip on the rock, but we were too cramped up. It was stuffy in there, and damp, and every sound was much too loud.

'Give us a bit of space, will you?' said Felix. 'Jessie, shine the torch for us.'

Kaia and Sarah went to the back of the cave, while we heaved.

'It's not coming, is it?' said Felix.

'Doesn't look like it,' I said. 'You got some magic

words, Kaia? Something from old O'Driscoll?'

'Move out,' said Kaia. 'I'll try.'

She put her arms round the rock touching the marks that the ancient people had left. She didn't try to pull it. She just held it.

After a while she let go.

'It won't open,' she said. 'Not for us anyway.'

'We'll get an iron bar,' said Felix. 'That'll shift it.' But he didn't sound very hopeful.

Outside, we talked about what we should do.

Sarah wanted to tell an adult – any adult really. She thought we were out of our depth. Felix was totally against telling adults anything on principle, because they always spoiled things. Jessie agreed with Felix – she thought we should blow the rock up with dynamite!

'Sarah's right,' I said. 'It's too hard for us, and I think we should tell someone, but not your mum. She's too busy with other things. I think we should tell the . . . er . . . ' I was trying to remember the word archaeologist. Kaia interrupted me.

'You mean the Oli!' she said.

Everybody laughed.

'That's it,' I said. 'The Oli! We should tell the Oli, because he knows about it.'

'That's stupid,' said Felix. 'He'll ruin it all.'

'What about you, Kaia?' said Sarah. 'You found this place. You haven't said anything yet.'

'I've been thinking,' said Kaia. 'And what I think is

that the O'Driscoll treasure is down those steps, and if we found it we could buy the whole island instead of it being sold for a holiday camp, and then we could all go on living here. We've just got to think of a way to move that rock, that's all. We can get iron bars. We can get ropes. We should try it at least. I say we give it one more day, and then we tell the Oli. Right?'

We didn't know it, but we didn't even have one day.

9
Counting Windows

We agreed to meet up again in an hour, then we went off to look for tools – an iron bar and some rope. Kaia went back to her camp and we went down to the house.

As we got there, Mary and Sean were just setting off for town.

'Sarah, you're in charge,' said Mary. 'We won't be long, and I've left some food on the table for you.'

It was potatoes and ham. They ate a lot of potatoes and ham. Felix swamped his potatoes with butter. It filled us up anyway.

Then Jessie and Sarah went out to see Sugar, the pony, and Felix and I went up to our bedroom.

Madonna lay in her cage, coiled up in a corner, sleeping peacefully.

'I still haven't worked out how she got into the boar's head,' said Felix, looking in on her. 'I'm thinking that little passage we saw must come right down to the house somehow, that's how she got back. So there must be an entrance from this end too.' He paused. 'I should think this house would be full of secret passages, wouldn't you?'

'There's something I've been thinking about, Felix,' I said. And I told him about the windows.

It was soon after I arrived, and I was on my own in the house. I'd already been looking at the windows. At home we have double glazing, and I'd never even seen a house like this one, where half the windows had cracked panes. I thought I'd write something about it in my letter home. And I started to wonder whether there were more windows with cracked panes than without. So I started counting.

I went round every room in the house. I was disappointed, because there were more windows without cracked panes. Just.

Then, to make sure, I went round the house from the outside. This wasn't so easy, because the woods came right up to the house in some places, and I had to clamber through a lot of brambles, but I managed it.

The only thing was, I counted one more window from the outside than from the inside. It wasn't cracked.

After that I forgot about it, until seeing Felix's snake climbing out of the boar's mouth set me wondering.

'That's grand,' said Felix, jumping up. 'That means there's a secret room somewhere. It's probably behind the old boar. Come on, let's look!'

We fetched the ladder and put it up next to the boar. Felix peered into its mouth, shining my torch.

'We're right!' he said. 'There's a little hole at the back there. It goes right into the wall. That's how she came through.'

'What's on the other side of the wall?' I asked.

Felix climbed back down the ladder and we both looked thoughtfully up at the old tusker.

'We're right in the middle of the house,' said Felix. 'The walls are really thick here. The other side of that... well, it wouldn't quite be Mum's bedroom, and it's not quite the passage...'

He stopped, his eyes lighting up.

'No, wait a minute! Come on, the library!'

The library was just below us. There were books all round the walls, but at the back there was a huge old inglenook fireplace.

We stood inside it and looked up into a dark empty space. The walls were rough, with good places to grip. I thought it wouldn't be too hard to climb up it.

'Somebody blocked off the top, otherwise you'd see light,' said Felix. 'You can't light a fire here now.'

Suddenly I had an idea.

'Felix,' I said, 'take the torch and shine it through the boar's mouth again.'

He knew what I meant, and ran up the stairs.

A moment later I saw a flicker of light in the darkness above me.

'Yeah!' I shouted. 'We've got it!'

Felix came straight back down, and stood in the inglenook holding the torch, while I climbed up. The first bit was tricky, but then it got easier, because there were bits of metal fixed into the walls at odd intervals, to grip on. It was dirty though. There were a lot of cobwebs.

It got darker as I went up further. I didn't look back down.

Then I came to a wide ledge. I pulled myself up and sat down with my legs hanging. I reckoned I must be about the same height as the old boar, that he'd be just the other side of the wall behind me.

I stood up on the ledge. It was bigger than I expected – like a little dark room halfway up the chimney. I swayed my head a bit, and suddenly I saw a pinpoint of grey light. I reached out towards it, and my hand felt a hole in the wall big enough to get my fist into.

'That's it,' I called down to Felix. 'I can see right through the boar's mouth here.'

I edged back, pushing my arm against the side of the chimney for balance, and nearly fell right over. There was no wall to push against.

'Felix!' I shouted. 'Can you get the torch up here? I think I've found something!'

‘Hang on there,’ said Felix: He ran out of the room, and I heard him clattering about on the stairs.

A minute later the top of the ladder appeared by my feet, followed by Felix’s head.

‘Why didn’t you think of that before?’ I said.

‘I did, but you’re the great climber, aren’t you?’ said Felix.

I helped him onto the ledge. Then I shone the torch at the wall beside us.

We had found what we were looking for.

10
The Oli Goes In

There was an archway in the side of the chimney, just about as wide as I was. And through it a spiral staircase led down. It was narrow, but not cramped like the tunnels on the hill. You could stand upright.

'You go first,' whispered Felix, nudging me.

I took the torch and stepped down. Then something brushed against my face. I stopped dead.

'What's the matter?' whispered Felix behind me.

'Only a cobweb!' I said. I brushed it off with my hand, and it stuck to my fingers. There was a little rustling noise below me. I flicked the torch beam down in time to catch the tail of a rat turning the corner.

I don't think Felix saw the rat, because he was listening to something from outside: a clatter from the cattle grid, and the crunch of car wheels on the gravel.

He groaned.

'That'll be Mum. Jeez, why does she always have to come back at the worst time?'

'What shall we do?' I said. A moment before I had been itching to explore the staircase, but now I was hoping for an excuse.

'If she sees the ladder she'll suss us,' said Felix.

'Okay, then let's put the ladder away. We can climb back up later.'

We hid the ladder just outside the back door. Then we looked at each other. Felix laughed.

'You're covered in cobwebs!'

'Perhaps we should clean ourselves up a bit,' I said.

We ran up to the bathroom, washed our faces, and had brushed off the worst of the grime, when Mary called us down to the kitchen.

She was too upset to notice our dirty clothes. She was fighting back the tears. She told us to sit down, while she unpacked some shopping. Sarah and Jessie came in too, and we all sat silently, waiting.

Mary gave us all a biscuit from her shopping. Then she stood with her back to the stove.

'I've got to tell you something,' she said.

She was finding it hard. Because she hadn't talked about it to us before, she thought we didn't know about what was going on. Actually we did know most of it, of course, but still had to pretend we didn't.

So she explained about why Desmond and Kathleen and Sean had to sell the house, and how it meant they'd have to move again.

'Is it definite?' asked Sarah. 'Can they still change their minds?'

We were all thinking: What if we find O'Driscoll's treasure?

'They're signing the papers today,' said Mary. 'Kathleen and Desmond are leaving tonight, and Kathleen wants the whole thing signed and finished with, right now. The people from CountryClub are in a hurry too. They're driving down from Dublin. They're all going to meet at the solicitor's office to sign the contract at 5 o'clock. So that's it, I'm afraid.'

She turned her back on us and fiddled with the kettle on the stove.

'I didn't think Sean would do that,' said Sarah. 'I thought he loved the house.'

Mary sighed and turned back to us.

'He doesn't have any choice really. He could have held it up a bit, but he's agreed to sign now because, if he does, Desmond and Kathleen have promised to give us some money from the sale, to help us move.

She paused.

'It's quite a lot of money. We'll be able to all get some nice things . . . '

'I don't care,' said Felix, looking at the table. 'I want to go on living here.'

'We all do,' said Mary. 'But we have to make the best of it. Now get on with you – I've got work to do.'

We went outside and stood together in a little knot on the gravel. I turned to Sarah.

'We've found something,' I said. 'We've found another entrance, from the house. It must join up with the tunnel in the souterraine, because that's how Felix's snake got down here.'

'Where?' asked Sarah, not quite believing.

'From the chimney in the library. You have to climb up inside . . .'

'Well show us! What are we waiting for?'

'Come on then,' said Felix, heading back inside.

'No, wait,' I said. 'Let's get Kaia.'

Felix looked puzzled.

'What do you want her for?' he asked.

'She's waiting for us on the hill. We were going to meet back there, remember? She started all this. She didn't have to show us the moving stone. It was her secret. But she did.'

'He's right,' said Sarah.

Kaia was sitting by the standing stone with her arms round her knees and her hair blowing back behind, staring into the wind.

'They've sold it,' she said when we came. 'That's what my dad says, it's already sold.'

We sat in the hollow where we'd had the fire – only

the night before last, but it seemed months ago – and told Kaia what we knew. I was just describing the staircase, when a figure appeared at the rim of the hollow and jumped down towards us.

It was the archaeologist – the 'Oli', as we called him. He was bubbling with enthusiasm.

'This place is amazing!' he said. 'You children are sitting on one of the great undiscovered sites of ancient history. We'll have to have a dig.'

Kaia was looking at me as if to ask me something, but I didn't know what.

'There's Stone Age and Iron Age remains all over the island. And an early Christian oratory that's been turned into a boathouse. It's a treasure house!'

He sat down.

'Nice to get out of the wind... You know, where we're sitting may have once been the burial chamber of one of the early kings of Munster...'

Kaia interrupted him.

'I think we ought to show you something,' she said.

Apart from the ancient marks, the flat stone still looked to me just like any other stone on that hillside, as we pushed through the gorse to get to it.

Kaia and I put our hands on the marks, and twisted the stone aside, revealing the tunnel.

The Oli was open-mouthed. But he wasn't looking at the tunnel. He was looking at the stone.

'Shut it again,' he said.

We pushed it shut and opened it a few times for him. Then he did it himself; he could do it on his own. He peered underneath it, to see how it swivelled on another stone below it.

'Marvellous!' he kept saying. 'That is absolutely brilliant. And you have to push in just that certain way or it won't work – it's all about the balance. That is Stone Age technology at its peak! Who knows, perhaps all the souterraines were protected by stones like this once upon a time, and this is the only survivor.'

At last he looked into the tunnel.

'So what secrets does the swivel-stone guard? A king's burial chamber, or an old grain store... A bit tight for me, eh? You'll have all been in, I expect?'

We nodded.

'Well I hope you didn't break anything or mess anything up...'

He took a big torch from his bag.

'I'll see if I can squeeze in...'

Felix was looking restless.

'We're busy,' he said. 'There's something we've got to do.'

We could see the Oli's back disappearing down the steps. He wasn't listening.

'Come on,' said Felix. 'We haven't got much time!'

11
The King's Room

We didn't mess about. We found the ladder and put it up inside the chimney and went up it one by one.

It felt a bit like Lemmings, the video game.

Mary was in the kitchen with the radio on. I think she was clearing out cupboards, and she didn't take any notice of us.

I gave my torch to Felix this time, and let him lead the way down the spiral staircase. We were making enough noise between us to scare off any rats, but there were still plenty of cobwebs to catch in our hair, and the staircase twisted around until we felt giddy. It seemed as if we were going deep into the earth. At last we stopped.

The torch beam showed a heavy wooden door, with iron studs in it. The bottom corner of it had been chewed away, showing light behind it.

Behind me, Jessie gave a little squeal of excitement. I couldn't guess what was behind that door, and my heart was beating like crazy.

'Go on,' said Kaia. 'Push it!'

Felix pushed. The door creaked and swung open.

The first thing I noticed was that there was daylight. It was grey and distant, but it seemed bright after the blackness of the stairs. It came from a shaft in the ceiling, like you get in blocks of flats sometimes. It was a long shaft, but at the top I could see there was a window letting in daylight. I thought, that's the extra window.

Then I looked around.

We were in a big room. The middle of it was lit by the shaft, but the corners were in deep shadow. It was all hung with old cobwebs, and crusted with dust, but it must have been nicely furnished once. There were a couple of ruined armchairs with the stuffing coming out of them, probably made into rats' nests. There was a sort of wooden throne at one end, set up on a stone slab, but rotten with woodworm and one leg half chewed away. There were some bits of what had once been carpets on the stone floor, and ragged tapestries hanging on the walls – faded and torn and well chewed by rodents.

In the middle of the room there was a big table, with big carved chairs round it. The table was in better shape than the other furniture down there, as if somebody had used it not that long ago. One of the chairs was pulled out, and on the table in front of it there were three things: a silver candle holder with a candle in it; a pen, and a writing pad.

We none of us spoke. It was very still and very silent down there. Not really frightening, just a sense of solemnity, like a church – the presence of the past enveloping us.

Still without speaking we went over to the table, and sat round on those big carved chairs.

Sarah sat in front of the writing pad. She looked at it, then picked it up, holding it carefully in both hands.

'It's a letter,' she said quietly. 'It's from Mr O'Driscoll. Shall I read it?'

'Light the candle first,' said Kaia.

Felix had a cigarette lighter. He lit the candle, which spread a yellow glow around our faces, but cast the corners of the room into deeper shadows. Then Sarah read:

Welcome to the King's Room!

Whoever finds this, finds three secrets and three treasures that have lain hidden for hundreds of years. Their time has come.

I am an old man, and my bones are becoming stiff. For many years I have come regularly to this room that was shown to me – and only to me – by my father, as his father had shown him. It is known as the King's Room, though some might call it a priest's hole, and has been the secret refuge of my family since the house was built. This is the last time I will clamber in here.

Under ancient Irish law, inheritance did not pass simply from father to son or nearest relative, but each generation chose its own chief to take the mantle of power and responsibility. Thus I leave it to my heirs to decide their own fate and the fate of the island. It is beyond my say now. Yet, in my old age, I find that what I care about most in this world is the sense of Spirit of Place – the spirit of this *place – something that few now understand. The English family camping in the wood have it, especially the daughter, and she would be my chosen heir, for what that's worth, English or not. We all came from somewhere else once. The wars are over and times change. In the end it is only love of the land that counts.*

Enough of that... You have found this room, whoever you may be, so you must know its secrets and treasures.

The first secret is the room itself. It was the dungeon of the ancient castle of the O'Driscolls that had stood in this place since time immemorial. When that was destroyed in the wars with Cromwell, my ancestors rebuilt this house from its stones, but they hid the entrance to this chamber, and it became the secret gathering place of Irish chieftains through all the years of war against the English Crown. It is an untouched memorial to the struggle of a thousand years, and in its own right a great treasure.

Who dug the tunnel that you will soon find, that was

the back entrance and way of escape? We will never know, but it leads through the burial chamber of the Munster Kings on the ancient, sacred hill of Inish na Ri. And that is the second secret and the second treasure.

The third secret lies beneath the throne of the High King. This may be the greatest treasure of all… Search for it!

Sarah put the letter down.

'That's it,' she said. 'It's just signed "O'Driscoll".'

12
The Tunnel

We all looked at the crumbling wooden throne. But there was nothing there. We went over to it and clustered round, looking for hiding places.

'Maybe he took it and hid it somewhere else at the last moment,' said Felix. We all felt disappointed.

'Maybe this isn't the throne,' said Kaia.

'I've found it! I've found it!'

It was Jessie. While we had been looking at the throne, she had been wandering round the room poking into the dark corners.

But it wasn't the treasure that she had found. She had found a doorway in the back wall, hidden by a decaying tapestry. There was a heavy oak door – it hadn't rotted, but the hinge that held it had, and it was hanging half open. Jessie slipped through easily and disappeared.

'Jessie, come back,' called Sarah. 'Wait for us. It might be dangerous in there . . . '

'It isn't dangerous!' Jessie called back. 'It's really exciting!'

By this time the rest of us were trying to get through the door. We were all bigger than Jessie, and had to squeeze through one by one into darkness. We could see the faint beam of Jessie's torch flashing around some way ahead of us.

'Jessie, wait!' called Sarah.

Felix came last. He'd been looking at the throne with his fingers on his chin, thinking.

This wasn't a tunnel; it was more like old cellars you keep coal and things in. We were in a corridor, with rooms on either side. I shone my torch in the first one. It was just an empty room.

'Creepy old place,' said Kaia beside me.

'Here it is!' shouted Jessie, ahead of us. Then her torch disappeared.

'Jessie,' shouted Sarah, her voice echoing around in the darkness. 'Come here now!'

There was no answer, and we started to hurry down the corridor. We couldn't hurry that much, though, in the dark. Sarah was a bit in front of the rest of us, flashing her torch around.

We soon found where Jessie had gone.

At the end of the corridor there was a rock wall. And cut into the rock there was the entrance to a tunnel.

Sarah was down on her knees, staring up it.

'Jessie,' she called. 'Don't be stupid. It isn't safe. Come back down here.'

'It is safe!' Jessie called back. Her voice sounded strange: echoey but distant. 'It's brilliant. There's steps and they just go up and up and up. I bet they go right up to the caves we found.'

'Come back here,' called Sarah. She sounded a little panicky.

'Okay, I'll wait for you,' said Jessie. 'Come on, it's great in here.'

Sarah was about to push into the tunnel. I put a hand on her shoulder.

'Let me go,' I said. 'I'm smaller. I can get up more easily. I'll persuade her to come back.'

'All right,' she said.

I had to go on my hands and knees to get through the entrance, but once I was in it was easier. The steps went up, then they turned, and then they went up again. After the turn I could see a dim flicker of light. It was Jessie.

'I'm glad you've got a torch,' she said. 'Mine's almost run out!'

I flashed mine up the tunnel ahead of us. We were nearly at the top of the steps. In front of us the passage levelled and turned again.

'We've got to go back, Jessie,' I said. 'It's too dangerous. What if a bit of rock fell down? We'd be stuck here for ever.'

'Oh, please!' said Jessie. 'Can't we just go a tiny bit further, please? Just round the next corner...'

'Do you promise you'll come back with me after that if we do?'

'Promise,' said Jessie solemnly.

'Okay, then. But I'll go in front.'

I squeezed past her, and led the way to the top of the steps, and round the next turn. Here the tunnel suddenly opened out into a sort of cave, and we could move freely. Then in front of us it narrowed again to a small hole; even Jessie would have had to crawl to get through it. I could imagine the ancient people waiting here to chop off their enemies' heads when they tried to come through.

We went up to the hole, knelt down, and I shone my torch in. It looked as though it opened up again on the other side, but I couldn't be sure.

'Can I go through? Please!' said Jessie. 'I'll tell you what it's like on the other side...'

'No!' I said firmly. Then I stopped, putting a finger to my mouth.

'Did you hear that?' I said. 'Listen!'

We both listened. Coming down the tunnel towards us, there was a faint sound, like somebody whistling.

It stopped. There was silence again. That complete silence you only get underground.

Then we heard footsteps. They were soft, rather shuffling, but definitely footsteps. Jessie gripped my arm.

'I'm scared,' she whispered. 'I want to go back!'

'Go on!' I whispered back. 'Sarah's at the bottom – tell them to wait in the King's Room. I'll come in a minute. And move quietly!'

As soon as she'd gone, I put my torch out and squatted down in the dark, ready to dash down the steps if I needed to. There were more sounds – shuffling and scraping and an occasional grunt as whoever or whatever it was pushed down the narrow tunnel ahead of me.

Suddenly the hole in front of me was lit up by a torch shone in from the other end. Then a large shape filled the hole, grunting louder and breathing heavily, with the torchlight flashing around as it tried to squeeze through.

This was it. This was the moment. I clicked on my torch...

...And shone it straight into the startled face of the Oli, who blinked in the unexpected light.

13
O'Driscoll's Treasure

'I should have guessed I'd find you lot at the bottom of the tunnel,' said the Oli. 'You seem to be one step ahead of me everywhere!'

We were in the King's Room. The Oli was dusting himself off after what had been a very tight squeeze.

'I should never have come down, of course. Far too dangerous on my own. I just couldn't resist though. Anyway, what have we here?'

He looked around.

'There's a letter,' said Sarah. 'From Mr O'Driscoll.'

'The old owner, you mean?' asked the Oli.

Sarah nodded.

'He wrote to me, you know...' the Oli continued, picking up the letter. Then he fell silent.

He read through it twice, and put it down.

'I see,' he said. 'So where is the third treasure?'

We all turned to the throne again.

'How did you move the stone that was blocking the tunnel at the top?' asked Felix suddenly.

'Good question,' said the Oli. 'I couldn't shift it at first, but I had a small crowbar with me, so I got that underneath it and lifted it, and it turned aside quite easily.'

'Have you got the crowbar now?' asked Felix. 'There seem to be a lot of moving stones round these parts. Maybe we could shift up this one the throne's on. It does say "underneath" the throne...'

'We mustn't disturb anything,' said the Oli. 'This is a unique archaeological site.'

Felix was already pulling at the throne. One of its arms came off in his hand, but the throne wasn't moving. 'Can you help me, Kaia?' he asked.

'You're pulling in the wrong place,' said Kaia. 'Try here!'

'No, no no,' said the Oli. 'Don't touch it! Look, you're breaking it!'

Taking no notice of him, Kaia and Felix tugged at the back of the throne, where the wood was solid. The Oli threw his hands in the air and moved over to try to stop them before they did any more damage. Then he stopped in his tracks.

As Kaia and Felix pulled the throne from the top, the

slab underneath it started to lift.

'Gently!' said the Oli, and instead of stopping them he helped them pull the throne right down sideways onto the floor. It had acted as a lever to pull up the slab beneath it, which, we now saw, was fixed at one side to two big hinges.

It revealed a compartment a couple of feet square – a hidey hole, no more. But inside it there was a small wooden chest.

We had found the third treasure!

Nobody spoke, not even Jessie. We had all dreamed of finding the O'Driscoll treasure and saving the island from the developers, but none of us really thought we would. I mean, that's what happens in books, not in real life. The Oli pulled the trunk out of its hole. It had iron bands across it, and brass handles, and looked just like you'd expect a treasure chest to look. It was quite heavy, too. It was definitely full of something.

The Oli put it on the table, in front of the candle which was still burning.

There was a catch on the front. The Oli shone his torch on it.

'It's locked,' he said. 'I don't suppose Mr O'Driscoll said where the key was, did he?' He smiled round at us.

'Yeah,' said Kaia. 'He did actually.' She was the other side of the table, and she held up a small brass key.

'He gave me this. He said he wanted me to have it. He didn't say why. He said something I didn't understand,

and told me to keep this till the time came. It was when he showed me the moving stone, the last time I saw him before he died.'

The Oli stepped back.

'Open it, Kaia,' he said. 'That's your right.'

She walked slowly round the table. Then she positioned the candle to give the best light. Then she slid the key into the lock. It fitted perfectly. She turned it...

I don't know quite what I was expecting...the glint of candlelight on gold coins, perhaps...diamonds and rubies, who knows? Or at least some ancient silver cross or goblet.

The catch flicked open. Kaia lifted the lid of the trunk, and we all pushed and peered over each other's shoulders to get a sight of it.

Kaia reached in...and took out a handful of old bits of paper, closely written in spidery handwriting.

Felix said something unprintable.

Sarah turned away. There was a tear in her eye.

'That's it then,' said Kaia. 'Old papers. What sort of treasure is that?'

But the Oli had picked up one of the bits of paper and was staring at it. 'This may be very important,' he was saying. 'If this is what it looks as if it is...We must move it all to somewhere clean and light.'

He put Mr O'Driscoll's letter on the top, and shut the trunk again.

'How do we get out of here?' he asked.

*

The Oli carried the box up the spiral staircase, while we trooped behind, still feeling disappointed. He put the box on his head to climb down the ladder, back into the library. We scrambled down after him.

He stopped dead at the bottom, blinking like a rabbit in a car's headlights. As we jumped down next to him we realised why.

Mary was standing with her back to the window and her hands on her hips, watching our progress. We were all covered in cobwebs and grime by now, and must have been a right sight, dropping down into the light.

'Is that all?' she asked as Sarah and Jessie came down behind us.

The next moment Kaia dropped down too.

'Well,' said Mary, looking oddly at the Oli, who seemed to be lost for words. 'You'd better fill me in.'

Jessie ran out to her.

'Mummy, Mummy,' she said, putting her arms round Mary's waist. Dirty arms they were, too. 'We've found a secret room and it's called the King's Room, and there's a tunnel and it goes up to the Monster Kings and we found the Oli coming the other way, and we thought we'd found treasure, but we haven't... '

The Oli found his tongue at last.

'It's tremendously exciting,' he said. 'Unique, totally unique. Your children have made a rare find... Can I put this box down somewhere?'

'I think you'd better,' said Mary.

14
A Race Against Time

The clock on the kitchen wall said 4.10. Mary made us wash our hands and faces first, and Felix and I spread some bread and jam. We were hungry. Jessie started showing Kaia the kittens. We were allowed to pick them up now.

'All right,' said Mary. 'You can all sit down and explain.'

It took a little time, with us all putting a bit in. The Oli was listening too, because he didn't know all of it.

Felix finished the story.

'So we thought we were going to get a load of jewels and things, and buy the island with them, but all we got was a box of old papers worth nothing.'

'There you're wrong,' said the Oli. 'From what I've seen these are certainly not worth nothing. Let's have a look now.'

He opened the box, and carefully took out a pile of manuscripts.

'I'm an archaeologist, not a historian, so I can't say for sure,' he continued. 'But if these are what I think...'

He took a sheet of paper from the top.

'This is from Mr O'Driscoll; it's a summary of contents...'

We watched him silently while he read. At last he put the paper down.

'This is astounding! These are records going back for four hundred years, and include first-hand accounts from some of the great leaders of the Irish resistance, starting with the O'Neill's own account of the Battle of Kinsale... It might be a forgery, of course, but if it's the real thing it's priceless! Priceless! And that's just the start of it. Four hundred years of hitherto unknown history in this little box! All that and a probable burial chamber of the Munster Kings too. You don't know what you're sitting on...'

He was getting very excited. But he put the papers back in their box.

'We mustn't touch anything any more. This one's for the experts.' He shut the lid.

'Are you saying those papers are worth a lot of money?' asked Mary.

'Money?' said the Oli. 'Oh yes, I suppose so. I

suppose there's plenty of rich Irishmen in America who'd pay a great deal for original manuscripts in the hand of the O'Neill, the last High King of Ireland. But that's not the point. The point is they should be in a university, being properly analysed . . .'

Mary interrupted him.

'The point is, I think, that there's three people who should know about all this, and they know nothing, and we've got until exactly five o'clock to tell them!'

She looked at the clock. It said 4.42.

'Get moving, all of you!' she said. 'We might just be in time.'

As we piled into the car, Kaia hung back.

'I don't want to go,' she said. I don't have a good feeling. It's your thing.'

'If you're not going I'm not going,' I said. 'It's more your thing than anybody's. The old man gave you the key, didn't he?'

'Come on, Kaia,' said Sarah.'We might save the island if we're in time.'

'We won't save anything if we don't leave now,' said Mary, starting the engine.

Kaia still looked doubtful, but she got in the back seat with Sarah and Jessie. Felix and I were crammed into the hatch with the trunk between us, bumping up and down as Mary went tearing over the cattle grid and down the drive, then over the hump-backed bridge and into the lanes that led to the town.

She was in a hurry. We skidded round a corner, and just missed a chicken that took off squawking and fluttering right over the top of the car. The sheepdogs tried to chase us as usual, but they didn't have a hope. There were no cars coming the other way, fortunately, or we might not have got there at all.

On the outskirts of town we joined a big road which was busy, and then we had to wait at some traffic lights. Mary was bent forward over the steering wheel. The Oli was shifting around in his seat.

Mary looked at her watch.

'Five minutes!' she said. 'Come on!'

But the lights were taking twice as long as usual that day, or so it seemed.

She headed right for the solicitor's office, but then there was nowhere to park. She had to go on round the one-way system, and ended up in the supermarket car park.

We piled out. The Oli took the trunk, and we ran up the road to the solicitor's, all pushing into the receptionist's little office.

She was just packing up to go home.

'What can I do for you?' she asked, eyeing us suspiciously.

'We're in a hurry,' said Mary. 'We have to see Mr O'Hara, right away.'

'I'm afraid Mr O'Hara's in a meeting right now,' the receptionist was saying, 'and I'm afraid he won't be available again until tomorrow morning...'

But Mary was taking no notice. She was heading for the stairs with the Oli behind her and the rest of us tagging along in a long straggly tail.

We burst into the room. We must have looked a sight, all breathless and still in our dirty clothes, and the Oli clutching a dirty old chest.

Six people were standing around a coffee table, looking as if they'd just stood up. There were Kathleen, Desmond and Sean, Mr O'Hara, the solicitor, and two smart men in suits, who looked up at us, startled.

'Hello, Mary,' said Mr O'Hara, smiling. 'What can I do for you? Will you join us for a drink?' He nodded over to his desk in the window, where a bottle of wine and some glasses were laid out.

'It's about the house,' said Mary. 'We've discovered something.'

She pushed the Oli forwards into the room, where he stood rather sheepishly holding the chest.

'This man's an archaeologist,' she said, 'and he and the children have found this box and a whole lot else.'

'I must stop you there,' Mr O'Hara said, 'because . . .'

But one of the men in suits interrupted him.

'No, no,' he said. 'Let's hear about this. It may be important.'

So the Oli told them.

There was a silence when he had finished. The suits were exchanging glances. Sean had his head in his hands. Kathleen had walked to the desk and was looking out of the window. Desmond had slumped in a chair looking at the ceiling.

'Thank you very much, all of you,' said one of the suits, picking up a file from the table. 'Thank you, Mr O'Hara, but we can't stay now. We have a long drive back to Dublin. We'll be in touch.'

Sean went over to Mary and took her hand.

'It's too late,' he said softly. 'We've already signed.'

15
Farewell to Inish na Ri

Kaia was by the standing stone, where I knew she'd be. The others were playing Monopoly, but I'd slipped away, out into the evening light, and up the hill.

We sat there together watching the seagulls flying home to their roosts. There wasn't much wind. Kaia's hair glowed reddish in the setting sun.

'We've got to go,' said Kaia after a long while. 'My dad got a letter.'

'Where'll you go?' I asked.

Kaia shrugged. 'Dunno. We'll stay here till they send the Guards in. This is our home.'

'Mary's been off looking for a house,' I said. Then, as

an afterthought, 'I'm going back to London on Monday.'

A kestrel swept over and hovered motionless in front of us, then suddenly dived and curled away.

'That's it then,' said Kaia. She picked up a little stone and threw it at a gorse bush. 'Nothing ever lasts, does it? Nothing good, I mean.'

I said nothing. I was thinking how I'd never come here again, because by next summer the house would be pulled down and the woods cut, and there'd be signs saying 'COUNTRYCLUB. PRIVATE. KEEP OUT!' And Kaia would be back on the roadside having rubbish thrown at her.

Kaia had her chin in her hands and she was gazing out to sea. Suddenly she stiffened, and reached out and took my arm.

'Look, Chris,' she said, an elation rising in her voice. 'Look!'

I looked where she pointed. There, past the cliff at the end of the island, where the ripples flickered red and gold in the sunset, I saw a small black triangle break the water and disappear again. Then another. And another. Then three together.

'It's the dolphins!' Kaia had come very close to me and was almost whispering in my ear. 'They come here sometimes. Not very often. Let's get closer!'

We ran together down the hill, past the beach where Felix and I hunted crabs, along a grassy lane between some scruffy fields, and out onto the headland at the bottom of the island where it met the open sea. There we lay on our fronts on the heather above the cliff, where the seagulls circled around us, and watched the darkening waters.

We were close now. We could see them well.

They made no sound as they broke the water, just the rhythmical turn of the fins rising and falling as the dolphins swam in a circle around the bay. Sometimes one would leap right out of the water and you would see its whole curving length as it slid smoothly back down into the waves. Once they came close in under the cliff and we saw the shapes of their great bodies beneath the water. It felt like they knew we were there, that they were performing for us. I thought, this is as magical as anything. This is as good as finding the King's Room or the souterraine. You don't get more magic than this, not on this planet.

Then suddenly they were gone. We waited and waited, scanning the water, thinking at any moment we'd see one of those fins breaking it again, while the sky turned mauve and the darkness closed in around us. But they didn't come back.

'You should come round and see our camp before you go,' said Kaia as we walked slowly back. 'Meet my mum and dad and my little brother. They're all right you know, really.'

'I'd like to,' I said.

I did go to see Kaia the next day, and Felix came with me. We sat round their fire while her mum fed the baby, and we felt awkward because it wasn't what we were used to. Then Kaia's dad started showing Felix martial arts, and we ended up having a great time and didn't want to go home. But we had to.

And two days later I was going home in another way, on an aeroplane back to London.

I didn't think much about Inish na Ri, once I was home. It made me sad to think about it, and I had plenty to do once school started. But about three weeks later I had a letter from Felix.

I didn't open it immediately. I kept it till I got home from school, and then took it up to my room to open quietly.

As I sat on the side of my bed with Felix's letter in my hand, all the memories of Inish na Ri flooded into me, and I thought, I should write all that down, I shouldn't let it all be forgotten. Then I opened the letter.

Dear Chris,

You wouldn't believe what's been happening here. It's been non-stop ever since you left. The Oli's been down a few times, and last Saturday he came with a whole group of people and they've put a big fence all round most of the hill, with a sign on it saying 'ARCHAEOLOGICAL SITE. KEEP OUT!' It says it in Irish too, just in case. So we can't go in there any more. I knew that would happen. Doesn't it make you sick? We're not allowed to go into the King's Room either, which is a bit much being as it was us that found it in the first place.

There's a good side to it though. The Oli says the whole island's being made into a 'Site of National Importance', or something like that, which means CountryClub people can't knock anything down. When they found out about that, they didn't want the island at all. Sean would've just let them off, but Kathleen said they'd have to pay compensation, and CountryClub are going to give them thousands of pounds! Anyway, the island isn't sold after all, and it seems like we'll be able to stay here. Mum says maybe there'll even be some money to do up the house a bit.

And you know those old bits of paper we found? They're going to be sold for loads of money! So it turns out they were treasure after all. I thought we could claim the money as we found the trunk, or at least Kaia could because Mr O'Driscoll gave her the key, but they say it's part of the house – like part of the furniture. Sean's been staying here for a while. He's going to pay his money to the others, so he'll just own the island by himself. Which would be grand.

I'm trying to get him to give me some money to buy a male snake to keep with Madonna. Then I can sell the babies. Kaia wants one. Would you like one?

It must be great in London. I've been talking to my mum, and she says maybe I could come and stay with you after Christmas if things are all right here and we don't have to move. Will you ask your mum? We'd have a great time, wouldn't we?

See you then,

Felix

P.S. I do Martial Arts with Kaia's dad every Monday evening. It's called Aikido, and it's ancient Japanese. Kaia's dad's brilliant. I never took any notice of him before, but he's a laugh when you get to know him. He's showing me about horses too, which I thought was boring before, because Sarah did it, but it isn't boring with him. Kaia's all right too, for a girl.

I put down the letter and thought for a while. Then I took my pen and an exercise book, and I started to write this story.

And now it's finished!